Bob
and the Big Plan

Illustrations by Craig Cameron

EGMONT

95% of the paper used in this book is recycled paper, the remaining 5% is an Egmont grade 5 paper that comes from well managed forests. For more information about Egmont's paper policy please visit www.egmont.co.uk/ethicalpublishing

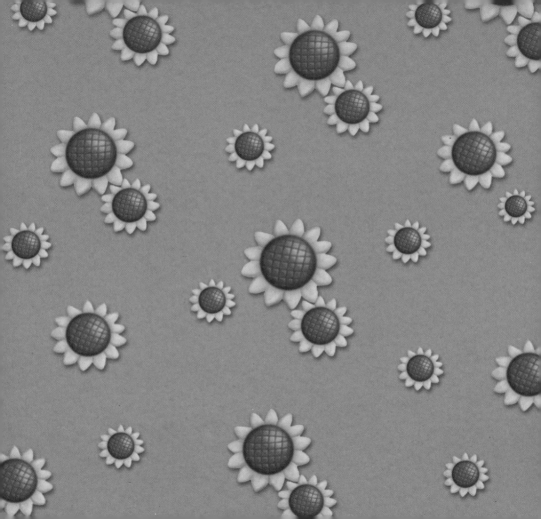

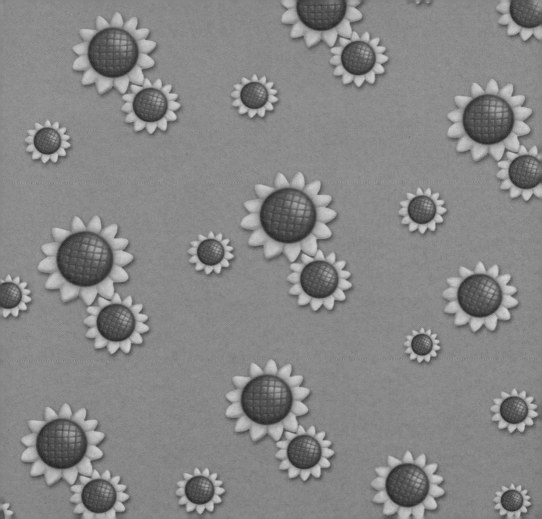

EGMONT

We bring stories to life

First published in Great Britain 2007
by Egmont UK Limited,
239 Kensington High Street, London W8 6SA

HIT entertainment

ISBN 978 1 4052 3142 8

1 3 5 7 9 10 8 6 4 2

Printed in Great Britain

When Bob hears about a competition to build Sunflower Valley, he faces his biggest building challenge yet. He's going to need a Big Plan . . .

Bob and the team were busy at work, building a bigger office for Mr Adams the architect.

"I'll need more space if I win the competition to plan a new town in Sunflower Valley," Mr Adams explained. "I've been working on my model for weeks!"

"We used to go to Sunflower Valley on holiday when I was young!" said Bob.

But Bob felt sad when he saw the model. Mr Adams had turned Sunflower Valley into a noisy city, packed with busy roads and big buildings.

"I'm taking this to the town hall, so everyone can have a good look," said Mr Adams. "The judging is the day after tomorrow. Goodbye, Bob!"

"Why don't you enter the competition, Bob?" asked Muck, later on.

"Great idea!" said Dizzy.

"Ho, ho! I'm a builder, not an architect like Mr Adams," said Bob. "And I have lots of work to do here."

Dizzy and Muck were disappointed. But the next morning, Bob changed his mind. He didn't want Sunflower Valley to be spoiled.

"What about the job here, Bob?" asked Scoop, sounding worried.

"Can you finish the foundations by yourselves?" said Bob. "The competition is tomorrow!"

"Can we build it?" said Scoop.

"Yes, we can!" chimed Roley and Muck.

"Er, yeah, I think so," added Lofty.

Back at the yard, Bob was looking through his books for ideas.

"Wow! Look at these buildings, Pilchard," said Bob. "I'll need a Big Plan to win this competition!"

"Miaow!" said Pilchard.

Later, Roley and Bird were watching Bob sketch his ideas for Sunflower Valley. But when Bob drew houses, they didn't look right.

"Toot, toot!" squawked Bird. He was showing Bob his nest.

"Good idea, Bird!" smiled Bob. "I'll have houses that don't spoil the countryside, like yours!"

"Brilliant!" said Roley.

Bob had almost finished his model, when he heard a noise outside. Vrrooom! Vrrooom!

Just then, Mr Bentley appeared on a shiny off-road vehicle. "Hello, Bob," he said. "I'm just taking Scrambler to the town hall – he's part of the prize for the competition!"

"Nice to meet you, Scrambler!" smiled Bob.

At Mr Adams' office, the team was in trouble. Dizzy was pouring out cement for the foundations, when Scoop noticed the markers were in the wrong place. Concrete spilled everywhere!

"Oh, no! What are we going to do?" worried Scoop.

"We'll have to fetch Bob before the concrete goes hard!" said Muck.

"We're really sorry, Bob," said Muck, when Bob arrived. "We made a mistake!"

"Now you won't have time to finish your model," sighed Dizzy.

"If we work quickly, we can move the concrete before it sets and use it later," said Bob, kindly.

"Reduce, reuse, recycle!" said the team. And they worked together until the job was done.

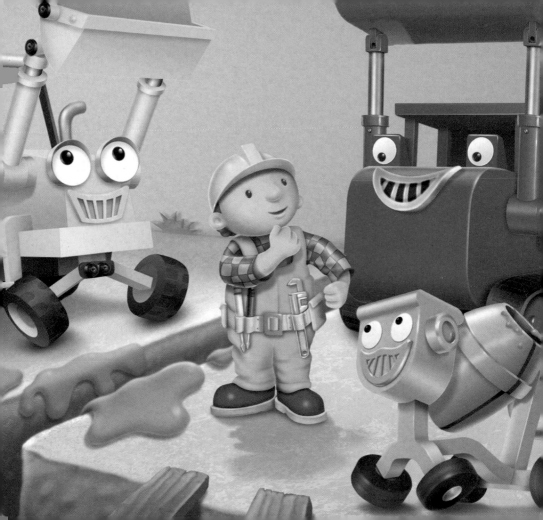

Bob had just arrived back in the yard when, suddenly, the lights went out.

"It's a power cut!" said Bob. "Fetch some lamps, Muck."

While Bob finished his model, he told the machines about the different ways to make power. "We'll use the sun and the wind to power Sunflower Valley!" he said.

"Wind turbines and solar panels! How cool!" said Scoop, excitedly.

The next day at the town hall, Mr Adams was finishing his speech when Bob appeared.

"Wait!" shouted Bob. "Here's my Big Plan for Sunflower Valley! We'd use recycled things to build a beautiful town," he explained. "Everything would be powered by water, wind and sun to save energy!"

"Ooh!" and "Wow!" went the crowd, when they saw Bob's model.

The judges looked at both models and nodded their heads.

"It gives me great pleasure to declare the winner and present him with Scrambler. It's . . . Bob the Builder!" said the Mayoress.

"We hope you'll plan and build Sunflower Valley!" said a judge.

Bob was very happy. "Welcome to the team, Scrambler!" he smiled. "Sunflower Valley, here we come!"

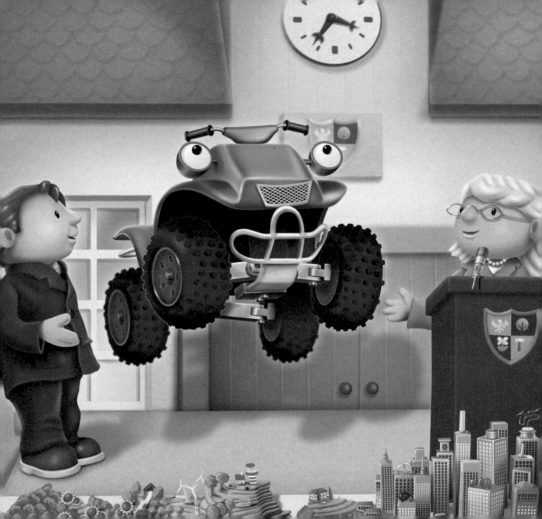

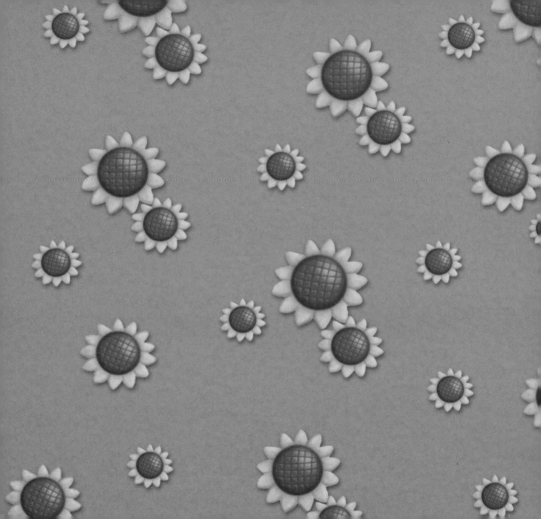